Disney PRINCESS

TALES to FINISH

COLOR YOUR OWN STORYBOOK COLLECTION!

Disney PRESS

Los Angeles • New York

All illustrations by the Disney Storybook Art Team

Printed in the United States of America

First Hardcover Edition, May 2017

3 5 7 9 10 8 6 4 2

FAC-038091-18323

ISBN 978-1-4847-8957-5

For more Disney Press fun, visit www.disneybooks.com

CONTENTS

Disney PRINCESS

TALES TO FINISH

Follow your favorite Disney Princesses on seven exciting adventures! Color in the art on every page, add the missing characters to the scenes, and create your own ending to each story to finish these enchanting tales your own way!

"**F**arewell, my love!" Snow White said. The Prince was leaving on a royal trip. It was the first time the newlyweds would be apart.

"I'll be home soon," the Prince replied. "In the meantime, I've left an envelope for you on the well. It's the first clue in a treasure hunt. At the end, you'll find a special gift!"

Draw the Prince on his horse!

The clue was in plain sight.
The Dwarfs gathered around
as Snow White opened the
envelope. "I wonder what the gift
will be?" she said. Then she read
the clue aloud:

Can't leave you a kiss,
Or even a hug,
So here is a clue:
Look under the . . .

"I know!" cried Sneezy. "The
Prince left the next clue under
a bug!" Sneezy quickly led
everyone to the garden.

7

Add some bugs to the scene!

Snow White and the Dwarfs looked under ladybugs, spiders, butterflies, beetles, and, very carefully, bumblebees. But they didn't find anything.

"Actually, it would be pretty hard to hide a clue under a bug," said Snow White. "Maybe it's hidden under something that *sounds* like bug?"

"Under a jug?" suggested Happy.

"No, he must have meant under a mug!" said Grumpy. "To the kitchen!"

But as the Dwarfs searched inside, Grumpy tripped over Dopey.

"Crawling on the floor in someone's castle is mad banners," scolded Doc. "I mean, it's bad manners!"

"Whatever are you doing, Dopey?" asked Snow White.

Dopey crawled out from under the carpet and held up an envelope.

Snow White clapped her hands with excitement. "Under the *rug*! Oh, Dopey, you're a genius!"

Snow White read the next clue:

Hooray, you found it! Easy when you try.
Now in the kitchen, just lift up the . . .

"Pie!" shouted all the Dwarfs at the same time. Searching had given them quite an appetite!

Sure enough, the next clue was hidden underneath a pie plate in the kitchen! Snow White served everyone a big piece of freshly baked gooseberry pie. Then, while they were eating, she read the next clue.

Put on a smile, it's no time to frown.
You'll find the next clue in your royal . . .

Snow White thought for a moment. "My royal gown?" she guessed. The Dwarfs all nodded in agreement and quickly finished their pie.

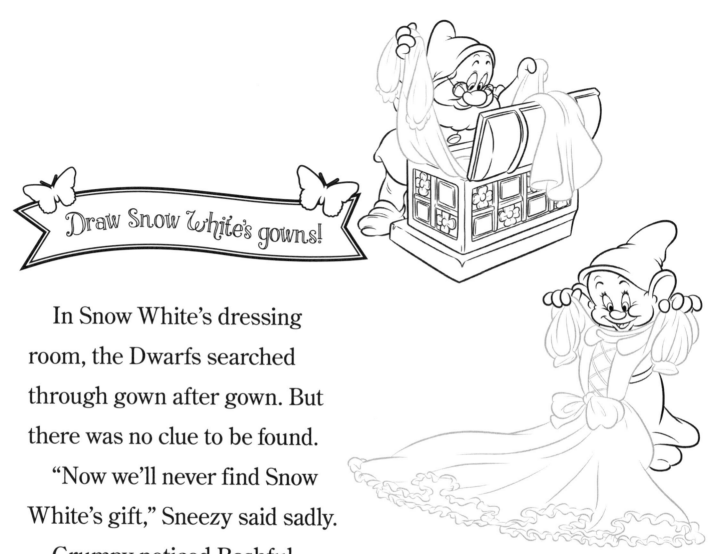

Draw Snow White's gowns!

In Snow White's dressing room, the Dwarfs searched through gown after gown. But there was no clue to be found.

"Now we'll never find Snow White's gift," Sneezy said sadly.

Grumpy noticed Bashful standing in the corner. "Why aren't you searching?" Grumpy asked him.

"Why, he doesn't have to," Snow White said. "He's wearing my royal crown. That must be where the clue is!"

Bashful took off the crown . . .

and inside was the clue!

The gift is almost yours.
My, my, this game has flown!
There's one thing left to do:
Go look upon your . . .

"Stone!" offered Sneezy.

"That's silly," said Grumpy. "It must be bone!" Soon all the Dwarfs were shouting out their own ideas.

"Cone!"

"Cologne!"

"Trombone!"

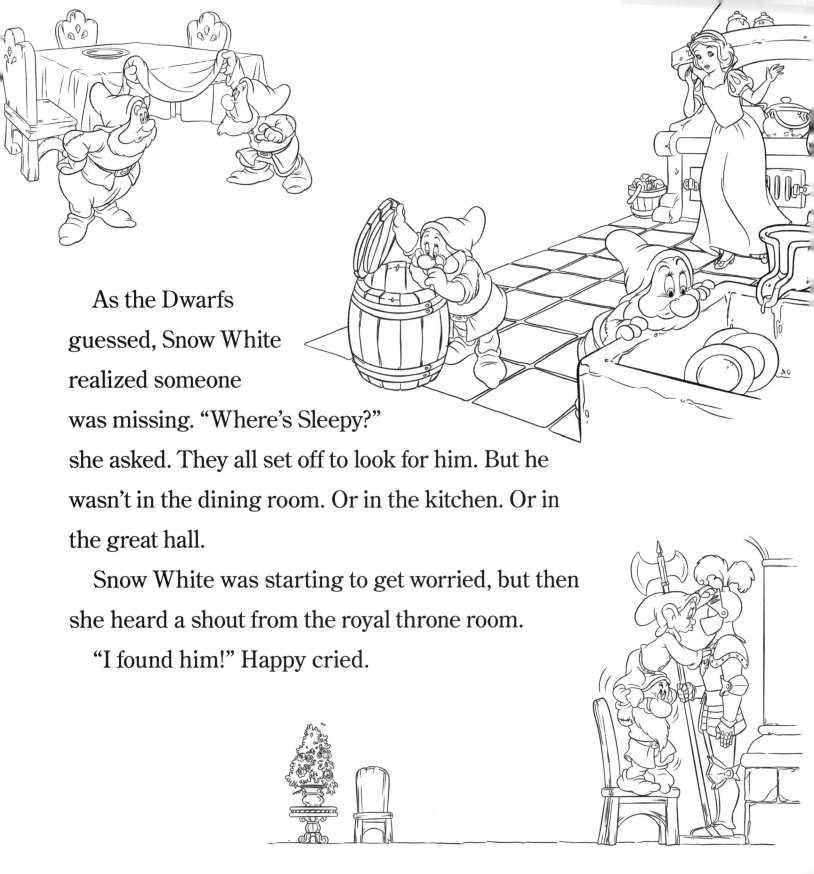

As the Dwarfs guessed, Snow White realized someone was missing. "Where's Sleepy?" she asked. They all set off to look for him. But he wasn't in the dining room. Or in the kitchen. Or in the great hall.

Snow White was starting to get worried, but then she heard a shout from the royal throne room.

"I found him!" Happy cried.

Sleepy was sound asleep on Snow White's throne.

"That's the answer to the clue," she whispered. "'Go look upon your throne.'"

"So where's the gift?" Grumpy grumped.

"Right there," said Doc. "Look!"

Sitting at the very top of Snow White's throne were two birds holding something that sparkled.

Draw Sleepy snoozing on Snow White's throne!

To everyone's surprise, the birds flew down and placed a
delicate necklace around Snow White's neck. The gift was a
stunning heart-shaped ruby on a golden chain.

"Why, it's the color of love," she said.

Doc saw that Snow White was holding something else. "The birds left a note!" he cried.

Snow White opened the envelope and read aloud:

Yes, jewels are lovely,
But as this hunt ends,
Keep one thought in mind:
The best gifts are . . .

"Odds and ends," said Sneezy.

"No, it's definitely chickens and hens," said Happy.

"Pens?" Bashful suggested quietly.

Draw the missing Dwarfs!

Grumpy couldn't believe his ears. "What's wrong with you fellas? The answer is 'friends'!"

"You're right," Snow White said.

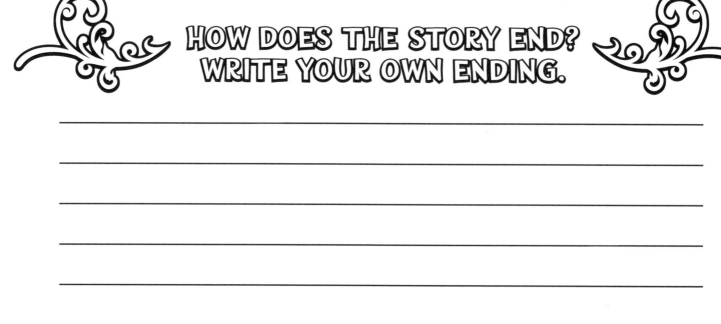

HOW DOES THE STORY END? WRITE YOUR OWN ENDING.

_____

_____

_____

_____

_____

Disney PRINCESS

Tangled

WANTED: Flynn Rider

WANTED
DEAD or ALIVE

Flynn Rider
THIEF

Princess Rapunzel and Flynn Rider were visiting their friends at the Snuggly Duckling. Hook Hand was teaching Rapunzel how to play the piano. Flynn was learning about interior design from Gunther.

Suddenly, the door flew open. It was the noble horse Max, followed by two royal guards. Max sadly held up a WANTED poster in his mouth. It had a picture of Flynn!

"Anyone else getting a sense of déjà vu?" Flynn asked.

"It looks like they think you stole my tiara again," Rapunzel said as she read the warrant for Flynn's arrest.

"What? I didn't do anything! Why does everyone always think it's me?" Flynn said.

Rapunzel just looked at him.

"Well, I guess they might have a few reasons," Flynn said.

The guards explained that late the night before, someone who looked just like Flynn had sneaked into the castle and stolen Rapunzel's tiara, right from underneath the guards' noses! There were witnesses all over town who said they had seen Flynn running away from the scene of the crime. The guards had no choice but to arrest Flynn.

"Don't worry," Rapunzel said. "We'll clear this whole thing up. You'll be back to interior designing in no time."

"Hurry," Flynn said as the guards led him away. "And don't let Gunther move the vase!"

The door shut behind Max, the guards, and Flynn.

"What are we going to do?" Hook Hand asked Rapunzel.

Rapunzel looked at all her friends in the Snuggly Duckling. She was worried. She knew Flynn hadn't stolen the tiara, but she would have to prove it. "Let's go back to town. It's time to investigate!" Rapunzel said.

Draw Flynn being taken away by the guards!

Later that day, Rapunzel and her friends reached Corona and questioned the townspeople. The town was abuzz with news and theories about the theft of the tiara.

"I heard that Flynn Rider stole it to give to a princess from a faraway land," a shopkeeper told Bruiser.

A baker said that he had heard Flynn was trading the tiara for his freedom from an evil magician. And a gardener said that Flynn was going to use the tiara to buy a ship and sail far, far away.

"He'd never do that," Rapunzel said. "He hates sailing."

Many people swore they had seen Flynn the night before. The librarian had spotted Flynn sneaking around by the paint shop. A sailor was sure he'd seen Flynn down by the docks.

"But how did you know it was him?" Rapunzel asked the sailor.

"The thief was wearing a green vest, just like Flynn always wears," the sailor said matter-of-factly. "Besides, he's stolen the tiara before."

"But he couldn't have been at the paint shop *and* the docks. They're on opposite sides of town, and there aren't two Flynns," Rapunzel said. "Plus, the last time he stole the tiara, he had help. . . ."

Rapunzel turned to her friends. She was starting to suspect who might really be behind the theft. But to clear Flynn's name, they would have to catch the true criminals.

"I think I have a plan," Rapunzel said, drawing everyone into a tight huddle. "Now, listen closely. . . ."

Draw Rapunzel and Pascal!

Rapunzel and her friends rushed to the castle to tell the King and Queen her plan.

"First I need the royal messengers to tell the town we're moving all the royal jewels to the throne room to protect them," Rapunzel said. "Then I need you to send Max and all his guards on an important mission out of town."

"But then everyone will know that the castle and all the jewels are undefended!" said the King and Queen together.

"Exactly." Rapunzel smiled.

The sun began to set, and the townspeople watched in amazement as Max led all his guards out of the city gates.

"They must be going to find the princess's tiara!" the gardener told the town librarian.

The royal messengers told everyone that the kingdom's jewels had all been moved to the castle's throne room. With everything in one place, the precious treasure would be easier to protect.

"Especially from evil magicians," the baker told the gardener.

Soon it was time for everyone in the castle to go to sleep. It had been a long, eventful day, and everyone was tired. Without any guards in the castle, there seemed to be no one to notice two shadowy figures crawling over the roof. And there were no guards to see those same two figures lower a rope into the dark throne room and slowly climb down. The thieves were back to steal the royal jewels!

The two people softly landed on the floor of the throne room. They quietly walked toward the center of the room, looking for the royal jewels. But the room was empty!

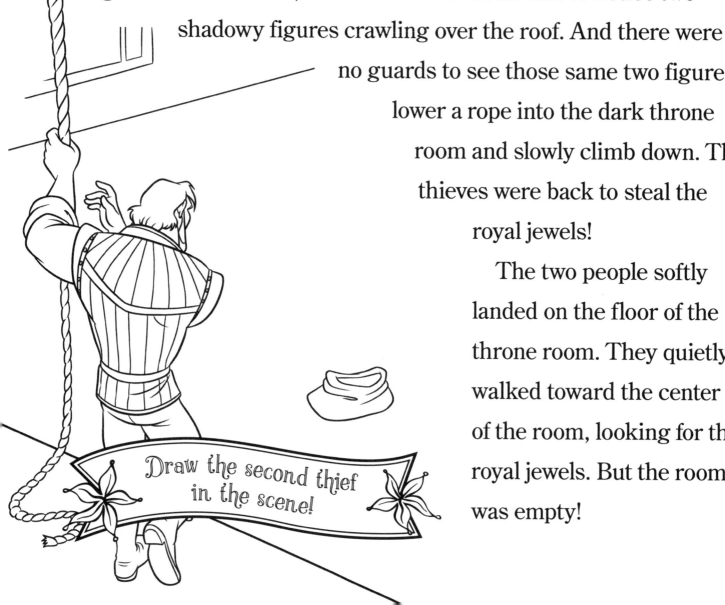

Draw the second thief in the scene!

"I don't understand," said a gruff voice. "Where are all the jewels?"

Suddenly, the room was full of light. Rapunzel and her friends ran out of hiding. It had been a trap all along!

Add the Stabbington brothers to the scene!

In the harsh light of her lantern, Rapunzel saw that the figures were dressed in matching green vests—just like Flynn's. But she wasn't fooled for a moment. As Atilla and Hook Hand restrained the criminals, Rapunzel removed their brown wigs to reveal . . . the Stabbington brothers!

"How did you know we'd be here?" the Stabbington brothers asked Rapunzel.

"I knew that the idea of getting more jewels would be too tempting for you to pass up," Rapunzel said. "Especially when you had seen all the guards leave the city. You didn't know that I had a scary group of thugs to help me out!"

Rapunzel explained to her friends how the Stabbington brothers had disguised themselves as Flynn to hide their true identities. That was why the townspeople had seen Flynn in so many different places. There had been two more of him!

"We knew that you would get to the bottom of this, Rapunzel," the Queen said, giving her daughter a hug.

Rapunzel smiled. "Now, if you'll excuse me, I have some business in the dungeon. . . ."

With Flynn's name cleared, Max and Rapunzel personally freed him from jail.

"I left the room warm for you," Flynn told the Stabbington brothers as Hook Hand and Vladamir locked them up.

Now there was only one mystery left to solve. "Where is my tiara?" Rapunzel asked the Stabbington brothers. "I can get my frying pan if I have to!"

"Boys, I'd be careful," Flynn said. "You do not want to be on the wrong end of Rapunzel's frying pan. Believe me. I know."

"It's right here!" said one of the brothers, pulling the tiara from beneath his vest. "After we stole all the jewels, we were planning to go to the docks and sail away to a faraway land."

"Not anymore," Flynn said as he took the tiara and placed it on Rapunzel's head. "That's better."

To celebrate solving the mystery, everyone went back to the Snuggly Duckling for a party.

"Be honest, you were a little nervous," Rapunzel said to Flynn.

HOW DOES THE STORY END? WRITE YOUR OWN ENDING.

_____

_____

_____

_____

BRAVE
Merida's Wild Ride

It was a soggy, stormy afternoon. Merida sat in the stables, reading from an old book of Highland tales. She and her horse, Angus, wanted to go for a ride—if only the weather would clear up.

"Look at this picture of a brownie," Merida said. "The book says they're little goblins who cause mischief unless you keep them well fed. Sounds like my brothers. . . ."

Angus snorted, shaking his head. It was clear that he wanted nothing to do with magical creatures, especially after their last encounter. Even though Merida had been able to transform her mum back from a bear to a human, Merida had learned that magic was not to be taken lightly.

Draw Merida's castle!

Merida read on until the raindrops slowed and the clouds began to scatter.

"Come, lad," said Merida to Angus. "The sun's breaking through. Let's go for a ride."

They galloped across the bridge and down the hill. But just as they reached the woods, Merida saw a flash of gray dart through the trees. "What was that?" she cried.

But Angus didn't want to follow it—whatever it was.

"Don't be a ninny," Merida chided him. "I'm sure it's not a bear." But what was it? Merida guided Angus into the woods, keeping her eyes open for another glimpse of the creature.

As they rode, Merida kept catching flashes of the animal. She urged Angus to go faster until they broke through the trees and into a clearing. There stood a magnificent gray horse. Its coat shimmered. Its mane was like fine silk.

Merida dismounted and approached the horse with a gentle smile.

Suddenly, Angus blocked Merida's path.

"Angus," she called, "don't be jealous, lad! This horse must be lost. We need to help him."

Merida cooed to the gray horse, and it responded with a soft whinny.

"See, Angus? He's friendly." Merida stroked the new horse's nose playfully. "Now I'll ride him back to the castle, and you follow close behind. Okay, Angus?"

Merida had a spare bridle in Angus's pack, but she decided not to use it. She didn't want to spook the horse with unfamiliar reins. Instead, Merida decided she could guide him with her hands wrapped in his mane.

Angus gave a resigned snort as Merida swung up onto the gray horse's back. But as soon as she mounted him, the horse reared wildly.

Add Angus to the scene!

Merida tried to calm the horse, but he started running. Faster and faster, the strange horse galloped until the field was far behind them. Soon the trees began to thin, and Merida gasped in horror. They were racing toward the edge of a cliff!

Merida tried everything she could to get the horse to stop, but nothing worked! She realized her only choice was to leap from the horse's back. But when she moved to jump, her hands were stuck in the horse's mane. His hair wasn't sticky or knotted, yet Merida could not free her hands. It was as if they were held there by magic!

Merida tried to slide off the side of the horse, but nothing could free her hands from his mane. She thought she was out of options. Then, suddenly, the runaway horse brushed against the trunk of a tree. Trapped rainwater fell down around Merida. Effortlessly, one of her hands came loose.

But Merida's other hand was still stuck. Merida did the only thing she could think of.

"Angus!" she cried. "Help!" Merida could only hope that her friend had heard her cry.

Merida looked up at the sound of a whinny. Angus galloped up next to them—and he was carrying the spare bridle in his mouth! He must have pulled it from his pack to help Merida.

Angus tossed it through the air just as they were nearing the cliff's edge. Merida caught it with her free hand and slipped it over the strange horse's head. As soon as the horse was bridled, Merida's trapped hand came free. With the reins, she turned the horse away from the steep drop-off.

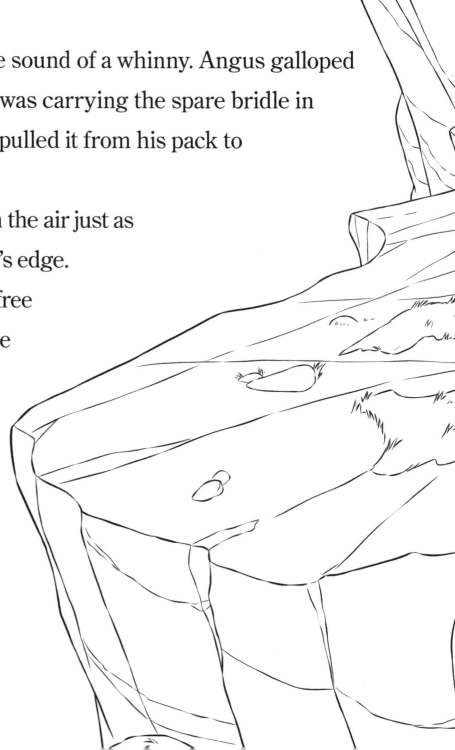

Draw the bridle Angus tosses to Merida!

Once the horse had calmed down, Merida guided him to a safe path beside the sea. As they reached the shore, the horse finally slowed to a stop. Grateful, Merida jumped off.

The stallion stood quietly. Merida looked in his eyes for an answer about what had caused the wild ride. It was clear to her that this was no ordinary horse. It must be a creature of magic.

Merida removed the bridle and whispered, "What are you?"

But the horse did not reply. He simply moved his head softly, as if he was nodding, before galloping down the shoreline and into the water.

Merida frowned as she watched him. As the horse raced deeper into the sea, he seemed to disappear into fog.

Merida mounted Angus and returned home. She was glad that the strange horse had not harmed her, but she wanted an explanation for her wild ride.

Back at the stable, Merida flipped through the book of Highland legends, looking for answers, until she saw a picture of a very familiar horse.

"Look!" She showed the book to Angus. "It's a kelpie. The book says 'Once a bridle is put on a kelpie, the water horse will do your bidding.'"

 HOW DOES THE STORY END?
WRITE YOUR OWN ENDING.

_____

_____

_____

_____

Disney PRINCESS

THE PRINCESS AND THE FROG

Tiana's Surprise Dinner Guest

It was a beautiful afternoon in New Orleans— the perfect day for some good food and good times with friends.

"Charlotte, honey!" Big Daddy LaBouff called to his daughter. "How about going to Tiana's Palace for supper tonight?"

"Oh, Daddy, that would be wonderful! Just give me a minute to change," Charlotte said as she ran off to her room.

A little later, they drove off. They didn't realize that their dog, Stella, was asleep in the back of the car!

Big Daddy LaBouff and Charlotte were always delighted when they walked into Tiana's restaurant. The whole place glowed with a warm light while Louis and the band belted out a great new jazz tune.

"Would you like to sit with my mama and Naveen's parents?" Tiana asked.

"Of course! We'd be delighted to," Big Daddy replied.

Draw Tiana's mother and Naveen's parents!

As the people she loved sat down together in her restaurant, Princess Tiana reflected on a memory of her father.

When Tiana was a little girl, her father had planned to open a restaurant someday, and it had always been important to him that it be a welcoming place where different kinds of people could gather together to share food and friendship. Princess Tiana smiled at the memory.

Meanwhile, Stella had woken up. She loved the smell of Tiana's beignets. She followed her nose right into the restaurant's kitchen.

"Lookee here!" shouted one of the cooks. "We have a visitor. Here you go, puppy— have some of this gumbo. It's a new recipe!"

Stella spent a happy evening in the kitchen. While Charlotte and Big Daddy dined to jazz music and talked with their friends, Stella was getting all kinds of treats.

At the end of the night, Prince Naveen's parents got ready to leave. They offered Eudora a ride home. Charlotte and Big Daddy had left a few minutes earlier, without Stella.

"Why, thank you," Eudora said. Turning to Princess Tiana, she said, "I have never heard the band play quite that well. And that new gumbo— absolutely delicious. I'll see you later, sweetheart."

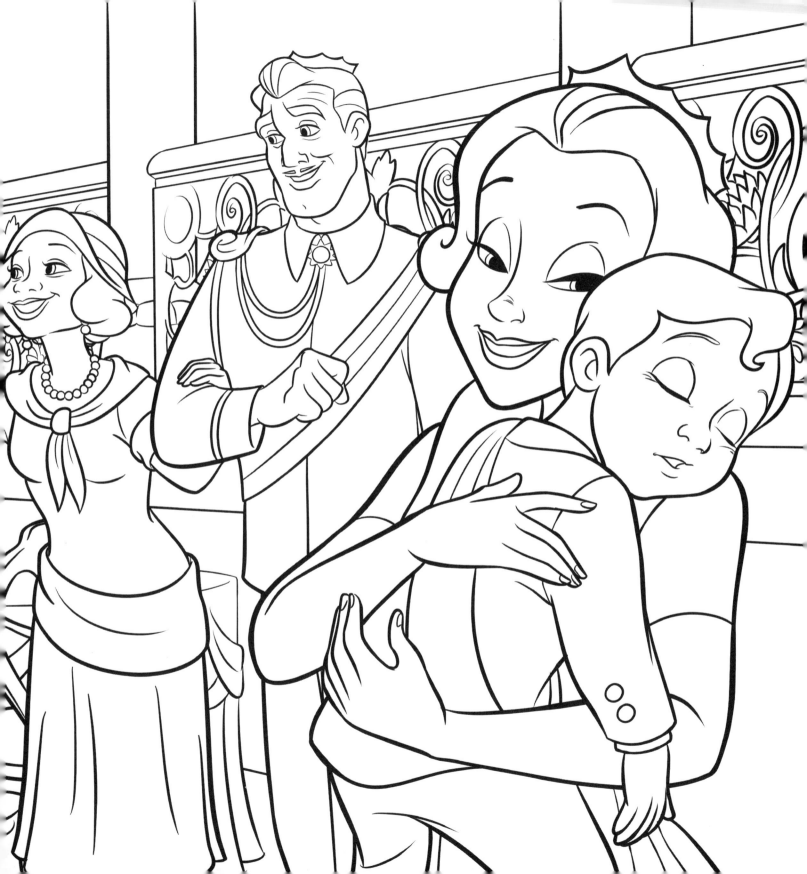

A few minutes later, Louis and the band began to pack up their instruments. It had been a long night, but they had played a great set.

"I don't know about you boys, but I could eat a horse!" Louis said. The musicians turned to him, shocked. Louis burst into laughter. "You know what I mean!"

Add Louis to the scene!

Add Stella to the scene!

They all followed Louis into the kitchen for their evening meal.

Grrr! Woof! Stella saw Louis enter the kitchen and was terrified of the giant alligator.

"Oh, now hold on, little dog!" Louis said to Stella. "I'm not here to eat you. I just wanted a taste of the chef's new gumbo!"

Tiana and Naveen heard the commotion. When they went to the kitchen, they saw that Stella was frightened. Tiana went to Stella and rubbed her fur lovingly.

"Stella, what are you doing?" Tiana asked. She petted the dog. "Don't worry. Louis is our friend. He wouldn't hurt anybody."

"That's true!" Naveen cried. "He is nothing but a big guy with a bigger heart."

To prove his point, Naveen widened Louis's smile with his hands into a big toothy grin that showed the gator's razor-sharp teeth. Stella still wasn't convinced.

"Aw, come on, Stella, I won't hurt ya!" Louis said. "I just want some of that fried chicken over there, just the same as you do."

Cautiously, Stella walked toward Louis.

Draw Naveen!

Once Stella realized Louis was harmless, she relaxed. Then she noticed the smell of the delicious fried chicken Louis was talking about. Stella wagged her tail and stared up at Tiana.

Tiana smiled. "Come on, Naveen. Help me with these leftovers. I think everyone deserves a good dinner tonight."

It didn't take long to pull together a supper of that evening's leftovers. Tiana even made some of her special beignets just for Stella.

The staff ate while Prince Naveen played the ukulele and Louis blew his horn. Everyone began to get up and dance to the music.

Before dawn, the prince and the princess dropped Stella back at Charlotte's house. No one had even noticed she was missing yet!

 HOW DOES THE STORY END?  WRITE YOUR OWN ENDING.

_____

_____

_____

_____

_____

Disney PRINCESS

THE LITTLE MERMAID

Ariel and the Whale Song

"**A**aaaaariel!" called a voice from beneath the brilliant blue water. Ariel dove into the sea and found her best friend, Flounder, waiting for her.

"Hello, Flounder," Ariel said cheerfully. "Isn't the water lovely today? Oh, you should come up to the surface. The sun feels so nice."

Flounder smiled and shook his head. "I think I'll stay down here," he said.

"Well, we should get back to Sebastian anyway," Ariel said, pushing her long red hair off her forehead. "I promised him I would sing at the concert today." Sebastian had organized a special concert for the first day of summer. Ariel was sure he'd be setting up for it already. She also knew that he would not be happy if she was late!

Ariel and Flounder swam side by side toward home. Ariel admired a beautiful coral reef as they passed it.

There are always new things to discover in the ocean, she thought. *I wonder if we'll have enough time to stop off at the shipwreck before—*

"Ah!" came a shout from behind her. Flounder was quivering and covering his eyes with his fins.

"Oh, Flounder, it's just a little crab," Ariel said, shaking her head softly. She swam over to her frightened friend. "Really, there's nothing to be afraid of!"

She peeled Flounder's fins away from his eyes as the crab scuttled away.

Flounder breathed a sigh of relief.

"We need to toughen you up a bit." Ariel smiled and gently prodded him with her elbow. She loved her friend, but even she knew he was a bit of a scaredy-fish.

Draw Flounder
being a scaredy-fish!

Draw the band!

Ariel and Flounder continued on and finally reached Sebastian, who was leading the orchestra through one of the final songs of the concert. Ariel wasn't that late. Why was Sebastian rushing through the rehearsal?

"Sebastian," Ariel said with a laugh, "slow down. We have plenty of time to get ready."

"But, Princess, we don't," Sebastian told her. "This isn't just a concert to celebrate the start of summer. It is also a concert we are performing for the whales."

"The whales?" Ariel asked.

"Yes. Don't you know? The whales are migrating through Coral Cove today. All of them! And I promised your father this concert would be timed exactly to their passing over us."

Sebastian chattered on, but Ariel had stopped listening. *The whales?* She would love to meet a whale. But how would she meet one if she was singing at the concert?

"And if this concert isn't perfect . . ." Sebastian was saying. "Ariel . . . Ariel?"

Ariel snapped out of her thoughts. "The concert *will* be perfect!" she assured him as she started to swim away.

"Where are you going?" Sebastian cried.

"I just need to get something from my treasure grotto," Ariel said, thinking quickly. "I promise I'll be back before the concert!" And with that, she swam off, with Flounder following close behind.

"All right, Flounder. Are you up for a quick trip to Coral Cove?" Ariel asked with a sly smile.

"Coral Cove? But . . . but why are you going there?" Flounder asked.

"To meet the whales," she told him. "They never visit us at the palace, so this is my only chance."

Soon they reached the edge of the reef, where Coral Cove began.

Even Ariel felt a little nervous entering the uncharted waters. And was it just her, or had the water actually gotten colder?

"I—I don't see any whales here," Flounder stammered.

"Me neither . . ." Ariel agreed, slightly disappointed.

She looked around, hoping to see some sort of sign. But instead of seeing a sign, she heard one.

Ariel listened carefully. The noise seemed to be coming from above. The more closely she listened, the more it sounded like a song!

"Flounder, follow me!" Ariel said excitedly. She swam quickly toward the brilliant blue light that broke through the ocean's surface.

The tune was getting louder. Just then, Flounder noticed a dark shape below them.

Ariel swam all the way up to the water's surface, hoping to find whatever was making the beautiful song. But as she looked around, she saw nothing but the wide, flat ocean.

She frowned, disappointed. "Oh, Flounder. There's nothing here," said Ariel. "And we need to get back for the concert soon or Sebastian will be upset with us. Flounder?" Ariel looked around. Where had her friend gone?

She was about to dive back under when Flounder suddenly burst into the air.

"It was—it was a shark!" Flounder cried. "A shark!"

Ariel tried to calm her friend. "Flounder, sharks don't come into these waters near Coral Cove, remember? It's too close to land for them," she told him.

Then she gasped. Something was approaching them, and it sure looked like a shark. Ariel dove beneath the waves to get a better look.

It came closer . . . and closer . . . until it was so close that Ariel could make out a giant tail.

But before she could figure out who the tail belonged to, it made a giant swooping motion, and an underwater wave surrounded Ariel and Flounder with bubbles!

When the bubbles cleared, Ariel was amazed at what she saw.

It was a mama whale and her baby. And they were singing!

"Whale song," Ariel whispered.

"It's beautiful," Flounder said, amazed—and also relieved there was no shark.

Ariel and Flounder floated next to the whales for a few moments, knowing they might never get that close again. Ariel listened carefully to the melody. Then she sang back to them. The whales smiled at her and continued to sing the tune, and Ariel joined in.

Suddenly, the two whales headed straight toward the ocean's surface and jumped into the air. They created a beautiful arc over the water and then belly flopped onto the smooth surface of the sea. The huge waves sent Ariel and Flounder soaring into the air. When they landed back in the water, they both had to catch their breath. Then they burst into laughter.

"That was pretty fun!" Flounder cried, still giggling. "Thanks for making me come along, Ariel."

Ariel smiled. It had been an amazing afternoon. But it was time to get back home.

Add Ariel and Flounder getting splashed by the waves!

Ariel and Flounder arrived just in time for the concert. When it was time for Ariel's solo, she decided to make a slight change.

HOW DOES THE STORY END? WRITE YOUR OWN ENDING.

_____

_____

_____

_____

_____

Beauty
AND THE BEAST

The Bedtime Story

The sun was setting over the Beast's castle. Outside, the world was snowy and cold. But inside, Belle felt quite cozy. Though she wouldn't have believed it possible when she'd first arrived, Belle was enjoying her time there. She had spent the last few days outside, taking her horse, Philippe, on strolls and even having snowball fights with the Beast.

Strangely, Belle was coming to think of the castle as home.

Belle watched through her window as the Beast walked

Philippe to the stables. Pausing, he gave the horse an awkward—

but kind—pat with his large paw. *There is more to him than meets*

the eye, Belle thought.

Suddenly, Chip bounced in. "Belle! Belle! " he called. "It's story time!"

"Now, now, Chip," Mrs. Potts said, coming in behind her son. "You must wait for Belle to offer to read you a story. Perhaps she is tired and wishes to go to bed."

"I'm all right," Belle replied, smiling. She'd gotten into the habit of reading bedtime stories with her new friends, and she'd been looking forward to it all day. "Let's go down to the library."

"Yippee!" Chip cried as he bounced out of the room.

96

Lumiere and Cogsworth were already in the library when the trio arrived. The pair had pulled Belle's favorite chair close to the crackling fire. A warm blanket rested over the back, and a thick book with a worn leather cover sat on the seat.

"I thought perhaps we could read this one tonight," Cogsworth suggested, pointing at the book.

Lumiere peered at the cover. *"Helmets through the Ages: A Detailed History of Headwear,"* he read aloud. "Ahh, no! There must be some excitement! Some drama! Perhaps some *l'amour*!"

"Let's read an adventure story! One with big, scary monsters!" Chip exclaimed.

"Nothing too scary, love," Mrs. Potts said gently. "You don't want to have nightmares."

Belle thought for a moment, her eyes skimming the colorful spines that lined the walls around them. Everyone wanted to read something so *different*. How would she find a story to make everyone happy?

Then Belle had an idea. "Why don't we make up our own bedtime story tonight?" she suggested.

"Our own story?" Chip asked, excited.

"Yes." Belle clapped her hands. "We'll go around in a circle and each add a line or two. It'll be fun!"

"A marvelous idea, dear," Mrs. Potts said.

"Magnifique!" Lumiere agreed.

"Quite!" Cogsworth added.

And so the friends gathered around the fire, eager to begin.

Everyone insisted that Belle go first.

"Okay," she agreed. She thought for a moment and then began. "Once upon a time, there was a knight named Sir Allard. He was noble and brave. Wherever he went, he rode upon his trusty steed." She smiled, thinking of Philippe.

"Did they fight dragons?" Chip shouted, bouncing eagerly.

Belle laughed at the teacup. "Why don't you go next and tell us?"

Draw the knight and his horse!

"Sir Allard went on lots of adventures. He fought big, scary dragons and saved lots of princesses," Chip said. "People came to his castle from all over to ask for his help."

"Ooh, I believe I have something to add," Cogsworth said.

"Wonderful!" Belle said encouragingly.

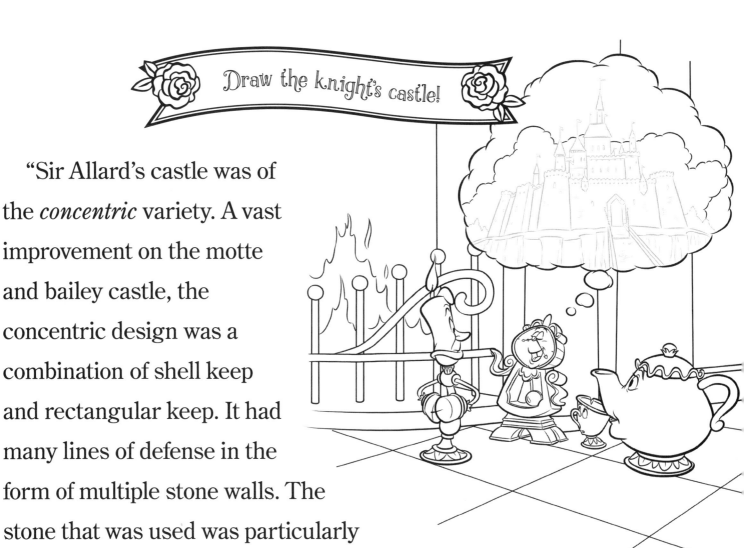

"Sir Allard's castle was of the *concentric* variety. A vast improvement on the motte and bailey castle, the concentric design was a combination of shell keep and rectangular keep. It had many lines of defense in the form of multiple stone walls. The stone that was used was particularly interesting . . ."

Cogsworth paused as he noticed Lumiere gesturing for him to finish his part.

"Well, yes, I suppose that was a few lines," Cogsworth sputtered.

"You gave us great details about the setting," Belle said kindly. "Lumiere, would you like to continue?"

103

"But of course," the candelabrum said. "One day, our hero, Sir Allard, heard about a ferocious dragon. And as all brave knights know, where there is a dragon, there is often a princess. And so, dreaming of rescuing the princess and finding true love, Sir Allard set off to find the dragon. He soon found himself in an enchanted forest—a forest that was so dreadfully dark that he could not see!"

"Ooh!" Mrs. Potts exclaimed. "I know what happens next!"

Draw Lumiere!

"As Sir Allard's eyes adjusted, he saw something large resting in the distance," Mrs. Potts said. "It appeared to be the dragon, but the creature didn't look like the knight thought he would. In fact, he looked a bit sad."

"What did he do, Mama?" Chip asked.

"Well, now, I've had my turn, Chip," Mrs. Potts said.

"We've all had our turns!" Cogsworth exclaimed. "Who will finish the tale?"

Suddenly, a cough came from just outside the library door. The group turned to see the Beast standing in the doorway. He had been listening to their story the whole time.

"Hello," Belle called. "Would you care to come in and help us finish the story?"

"No," the Beast said gruffly, turning to leave. "I wouldn't know what to say. . . ."

"Ah, you can do it," Lumiere said.

"It's easy!" Chip added.

"Please," Belle said, motioning for him to sit next to her.

"All right." The Beast strode over and sat next to Belle. "Well, I thought that . . . maybe . . . I don't know. This is ridiculous," he said, fidgeting nervously.

Belle put her hand on his paw and smiled encouragingly. He looked at it and then tried again. "The knight saw that the dragon was upset . . . and lonely . . . so Sir Allard talked to him. And something very unlikely happened—the two of them became . . . well . . . friends. The end."

The room was quiet for a moment. Then everyone began to speak at once.

"Très bien!" Lumiere exclaimed.

"Splendid, sir!" Cogsworth cried.

Belle smiled.

 HOW DOES THE STORY END? WRITE YOUR OWN ENDING.

_____

_____

_____

_____

_____

Cinderella

The Great Cat-tastrophe

Cinderella stood in the dining room, carefully arranging fresh flowers.

"Beeea-autiful, Cinderelly!" her mouse friend Jaq said.

Cinderella smiled. "I just adore flowers," she said. Then she sighed. "I wish I could go to the flower show tomorrow."

Once a year, the King hosted the Royal Flower Show for the village. Many unusual flowers would be on display. But Cinderella's stepmother, Lady Tremaine, never allowed her to go.

Just then, Lady Tremaine appeared in the doorway.

"Cinderella," Lady Tremain said sternly. "What did I hear you say?"

"Well—I . . ." Cinderella began.

Lady Tremaine held up her hand. Then an odd smile crossed her face. "So, you want to go to the Royal Flower Show? Well, I see no reason why you can't, as long as you finish all your chores today."

Add the evil stepsisters to the scene!

"Do you mean it, Stepmother?" Cinderella said excitedly. "Oh, thank you!"

Cinderella still had to scrub the floors, wash the clothes, and dust the furniture. But she was sure she could finish everything before the end of the day.

Just then, a fancy carriage pulled up in front of the house. Cinderella's stepsister Drizella shoved her other stepsister, Anastasia, aside so she could be out the door first.

"Girls, your manners!" Lady Tremaine cried. Then she turned to Cinderella. "Oh, I forgot to mention that the girls and I are taking Lady DuPont out for the day. Everything must be finished before we return at five o'clock. And dinner must be ready, too."

Before Cinderella could answer, a footman walked up and handed Cinderella two fluffy cats.

Lady Tremaine smiled. "And you will also be watching Lady DuPont's cats, Precious and Treasure."

Cinderella brought the two cats to the sitting room. Lucifer, the family cat, followed her. Cinderella gently placed the pets on the sofa.

"How much trouble could two sweet little kitty cats be?" she said.

Then Cinderella went to work. She quickly dusted the furniture and scrubbed the floor. Next she headed to the kitchen and popped a roast into the oven. While it cooked, she went outside to wash the clothes.

"All done!" she said as she hung the last piece to dry. "Now I'll just check on the cats."

Draw the two cats on the couch!

115

"Precious? Treasure? Lucifer?" Cinderella called, opening the sitting room door. "Are you awake . . . ? Oh, no!" she cried. The sitting room was a disaster!

Feathers had been ripped from the pillows. The drapes were tangled. And dusty paw prints covered every inch of the floor Cinderella had just cleaned.

"Come here, you little troublemakers," Cinderella said as she caught Precious and Treasure in her arms.

The cats didn't care that they had made such a big mess. Now Cinderella would never make it to the Royal Flower Show.

"Don't you two have any manners?" Cinderella said. With all eight paws, the cats wrestled from her grip.

Cinderella sighed as she restuffed the pillows and straightened the drapes. Soon the room looked almost normal. But the footprints were still everywhere. She would never be able to clean them all in time. Then Cinderella had an idea.

In a flash, Cinderella had sewn tiny mop shoes for the cats to wear! Once she had fitted the shoes over their paws, she found a ball of yarn and tossed it onto the floor. The cats began chasing it around the room. Their shoes dusted the floor and furniture as they went, without them even knowing it.

In no time, the paw prints were gone.

With the cats busy chasing the yarn, Cinderella went to check on dinner. Delicious smells filled the kitchen. The roast and vegetables were almost done. "Now all I have to do is keep an eye on the cats until everyone's home," she said, "and I'll be able to go to the flower show for sure!"

When Cinderella returned from the kitchen, she found the cats innocently napping on a windowsill in the warm afternoon sunlight.

"There you are," she said. The cats looked peaceful enough. But Lucifer was hiding something under his paw. Cinderella took a closer look. It was Jaq's hat!

"Lucifer, what have you done with Jaq?" she demanded.

The three cats snickered and glanced out the window. Cinderella gasped. The mice were huddled out on the roof.

"Oh, you mean things!" Cinderella scolded the cats. "You chased them out there, didn't you?"

Draw Jaq and Gus on the roof!

Cinderella could see that the mice were too frightened to move. She needed to rescue her friends! After propping the window open, she carefully climbed onto the roof. She held on to a tree branch and made her way toward the mice.

This isn't so bad, she thought. *It's almost like how I used to climb trees when I was a girl. I just won't look down.*

"I'm coming!" she told the mice. "Don't be scared!" She reached out to them.

"Cinderelly to the rescue!" squeaked the mice.

They sighed in relief once Cinderella had placed them in her apron pocket. But just as Cinderella turned, she heard a loud noise behind her. *Snap!*

The cats had locked the window shut!

"What are we going to do now?" groaned Jaq.

Cinderella was stuck. There were no other windows she could reach. And the roof was too steep to climb down.

Bong! The castle clock began to chime. It was five o'clock. Lady Tremaine would be home any minute—and dinner was about to burn!

Just then, Cinderella noticed the clothesline she had used earlier still attached to the windowsill. It stretched all the way to a tall tree in the yard. That gave her an idea.

"Everybody hold on tight!" she said to the mice. She took off her apron and looped it around the clothesline. "Next stop: the kitchen!"

By the time Lady Tremaine, Drizella, Anastasia, and Lady DuPont arrived, Cinderella was just placing dinner on the table.

HOW DOES THE STORY END? WRITE YOUR OWN ENDING.

_____

_____

_____

_____

_____